through the window of
WINTER the RABBIT

Written by | Illustrated by
Janea D. Harris | **Kimiyo Nishio**

Printed in the United States of America
First Printing, 2020

ISBN 978-1-7334092-7-8

www.Supherbooks.com

Dedication

Dedicated to all the children
who are bravely adapting to life during the pandemic and
the family and friends who love and support them.

If you pass by my window, you just might find,
Me, Winter the Rabbit looking out from inside.

Ruby Racoon quickly spots me, she turns, and she shouts, "Come out and join us, we're ready to play," but tucked safely inside is where I must stay.

I give a big smile and wave, though I feel a little sad,
I can't help but think of all the fun that we've had.

I miss high fives and hugs and laughing loud as can be. Even though I'm inside, my friends haven't forgotten about me.

I miss reading with Teacher Heather,
she is the best. I miss learning math with Teacher Eric
in his polka dot vest.

I am filling my days with activities both new and old, I am practicing hip-hop dancing

and painting using colors
so cheery and bold.

I love being creative and sometimes get lost in my dreams, I dream of playing tag and joining friends for ice cream.

I peek out of my window and I am so surprised to see, Sam the squirrel and Cami the chipmunk bringing special treats just for me!

I am so happy to see them and
oh how I wish that I could go out and play,
Seeing them through my window
has brightened my day.

Lady the Lama is my best friend indeed,
She sits at my window and sews the masks
we all need.

She makes me laugh and giggle with
the stories that she tells,
She always shows empathy and she listens so well.

Lady Lama's knit creations are simply divine,
She makes hats in blue, green and yellow but the red
is all mine.

We will all be together soon, learning, laughing and playing in school once again.
For now, I'll look through my window for special visits, from special friends.

The Author

Janea D. Harris is an author and poet who loves using creative writing to help children gain a better understanding of complex topics. As an educator, she learned that children often discover lasting life-long lessons in the books that they read when they are very young. When she is not writing, she volunteers her time to various education and community-based organizations. Janea lives with her husband, daughter and son on the North Shore of Chicago, IL.

Illustrator

Kimiyo Nishio is an Illustrator/Concept Artist based in sunny Los Angeles, California. She is a dog lover, foodie, anime fan and a mother of a 4-year-old daughter. Her adventures in motherhood keep her inspired and passionate about creating quality work, especially for women and children.

Made in the USA
Middletown, DE
28 October 2020